Word List

Here is a list of words that might make it easier to read this book. You'll find them in boldface the first time they appear in the story.

Mariko	MAR-i-koh
Kyoto	kee-OH-toh
filmmakers	FILM-may-kers
documentary	do-kyuh-MEN-tuh-ree
Cha-Doh	CHO-doh
koi	koy
translated	trans-LAY-tid
alcove	AL-kohv
kimono	kee-MOH-noh
Tomio	TOH-mee-oh
ceramic	suh-RA-mik
Arigato	AR-ee-go-toh
honorable	O-ner-uh-buhl
calligraphy	kuh-LI-gruh-fee
haiku	HEYE-koo
Hiro	HEAR-oh
Tokyo	TOH-kee-oh
Sushi	SOO-shee
observations	ob-ser-VAY-shuns
Takayama	TA-kuh-yo-muh
desperate	DES-pruht
vinegared	VI-ni-gerd

Barbie™

Mystery of the Emperor's Teapot

BARBIE and associated trademarks are owned by and used under license from Mattel, Inc. © 1999 Mattel, Inc. All Rights Reserved. Published by Grolier Books, a division of Grolier Enterprises, Inc. Story by Jacqueline A. Ball. Photo crew: Tom Wolfson, Patrick Kittel, Richard Brandt, Dave Bateman, Lin Carlson, Susan Cracraft, Machiko Tanaka, Mark Adams, Lisa Collins, and Judy Tsuno. Produced by Bumpy Slide Books. Printed in the United States of America. ISBN: 0-7172-8893-5

G
GROLIER
B O O K S

Barbie aimed her camera at the lovely sight across the pond. "Just one more picture, Kira," she said. "I want to photograph how the teahouse looks reflected in the water."

"Okay, Barbie," Kira agreed. "Then can we please photograph how it looks from the inside? Maybe while we're eating?"

Barbie chuckled. "All right, all right. I'm hungry, too. Besides, you must be looking forward to catching up with your old friend."

"Old friend and distant cousin," Kira corrected. "And you're right, I'm so excited!

I haven't seen **Mariko** in years. The last time was when my family was vacationing in Japan. Mariko was thrilled when I told her we would be working in **Kyoto** for a couple of days." She glanced at her watch. "In fact, we'd better get going. She'll be waiting."

Filmmakers Barbie and Kira were in the beautiful, old city of Kyoto, Japan. They were looking at possible places to film a **documentary** The fact-filled movie would be about Japanese customs and traditions. A large part of the film would show the ancient Japanese tea ceremony. There were certain rules to follow and special cups, bowls, and utensils to use. The Japanese call the ceremony *Cha-Doh,* which means "The Way of Tea."

Barbie zipped her camera into its case. "All done. Now we can go and eat—and hear that teapot story you mentioned on the plane."

"I can't remember the whole thing," replied

Kira, "but Mariko will. Her family is bursting with pride about that teapot."

They crossed one of the wooden footbridges over the pond. Something gold sparkled up at them from under the water.

"There must be a lot of **koi** down there to shine so brightly," Kira said. Large fish called koi were often found in ponds in Japanese gardens.

On the other side, they followed a path of round stones set into the ground. The path led them through the garden and then to the teahouse. A sign written in Japanese characters hung next to the front door.

"Inn of Ten Blessings," Kira **translated.** She was Japanese-American and could read and write Japanese as well as English.

"Which ten blessings?" asked Barbie. "Are they part of the teapot story?"

"You'll have to wait and hear for yourself," Kira answered, smiling.

They stepped into a large space that had been divided into two parts. One part was modern and open. Customers sat in comfortable-looking chairs at large wooden tables, chatting and drinking tea. Waitresses hurried across the wide wooden floor, carrying bowls of noodles and plates of tiny cakes

The other part seemed to belong to an ancient world. It was screened off by sliding panels covered with white rice paper. Pairs of shoes, toes pointing out, were lined up outside the closed panels.

Through the thin white paper, Barbie could make out the shadows of people inside. They were sitting on the floor. Their voices drifted outside.

"This is amazing!" Barbie exclaimed. "It's like being in two worlds at once." Her eyes wandered around the room and then fixed on something. "I guess that's the place of honor."

She was looking at an **alcove,** a special display area set into the wall. A shelf held a large, white vase full of purple and white orchids. Next to the vase, resting on a wooden block, was an old iron teapot.

"Right you are," said Kira. "And that's the famous teapot."

They moved closer to the alcove. The teapot was battered and blackened, as if it had been in a fire. It had no lid. But like so many Japanese things, there was something soothing about its style. Barbie felt peaceful just standing near it.

"Kira?" called a voice behind them. They turned to see a lovely young woman rushing toward them. Her dark hair was piled on top of her head, and she wore a lavender **kimono.**

"Mariko?" said Kira. The two cousins stared at each other. "You look so grown-up!" they both cried at the same time. Then they burst into laughter and jumped up and down with excitement.

"Barbie, this is Mariko," Kira introduced.

"Hello, Mariko," Barbie greeted her. "I'm happy to meet you."

Mariko's smile was warm and friendly as she bowed and clasped Barbie's hand. "I feel as if I know you already through Kira's letters, Barbie. Come, let's have some tea."

They sat down at one of the big wooden tables. Instantly a waitress appeared. Mariko spok briefly to her in Japanese. The waitress hurried of

"We have a lot of catching up to do, Mariko Kira said. She put her arm around her friend's shoulders. "But first I want to compliment you on your lovely teahouse and garden. Barbie and I really love the arched footbridges and pond full of sparkling goldfish."

"Thank you, Kira," replied Mariko. "All of our koi are dark and speckled. But the water does

seem to sparkle since we had the pond cleaned last week."

"I promised Barbie you would tell her the story of the teapot," Kira began. "Would you mind?"

Mariko nodded and smiled. "Telling the story is always a great pleasure. It begins late one night, many years ago. A young man named **Tomio** was walking through the old village that used to be here. Suddenly he saw flames burst out of a house. The fire quickly spread. Soon all the houses in the village were blazing!

"Tomio banged on doors, shouting at people to wake up and get outside. He checked to be sure that everyone was safe. At the last house, he saw a young woman struggling to help an older woman out of the house. Tomio ran in. He carried out the grandmother, who could not walk. No sooner had the granddaughter escaped than the whole row of houses collapsed."

Quickly, the waitress set down a tray. She

poured hot water from an iron teapot into large, colorful **ceramic** cups. Then she added scoops of a greenish powder. This special powder was made from dried, ground tea leaves.

"*Arigato,* Teri," Mariko said, thanking the waitress. She stirred the tea with a bamboo whisk and turned back to her guests. "I hope you like our green tea," Mariko added and continued with the story. "The next morning, the grandmother found her teapot poking out of the ashes. It was badly damaged, but it was all she had left. She gave it to Tomio, telling him it had blessed her family for generations. She said it would bring him good luck wherever he went. But by then, Tomio knew he was not going anywhere! He had fallen in love with her granddaughter. Soon afterward they married. Together, they built this teahouse and named it the Inn of Ten Blessings. As luck would have it, they later had ten children. The teapot has been here ever since." Mariko smiled. "Tomio was my ancestor, and this is the teahouse of my **honorable** family."

"What a wonderful story!" cried Barbie. "You must be very proud of your brave ancestor."

"Yes, we are proud," Mariko replied. "And the teapot still brings us good fortune—and good business. People come from far away to see it and feel inspired by it." She laughed. "In fact, so many people come that sometimes we run out of tea and cakes! We have enough customers to be open day and night. We have been thinking about serving meals and becoming a full-scale restaurant."

"That's terrific," Barbie declared. "But I noticed the teapot had no lid. Was it lost in the fire?"

Mariko shook her head. "We do not know the answer to that question. My family has never seen the lid. Some experts say the teapot may be an emperor's, but without a lid, we will never know." With that, she got up gracefully. "And now let me find my father. He is looking forward to seeing you again, Kira, and to meeting Barbie."

Barbie and Kira finished their tea and cakes and wandered over to the teapot. Something lying on the floor caught Barbie's eye. She knelt down to pick it up. It was a piece of paper covered with Japanese characters. They were beautifully formed.

"What amazing **calligraphy**!" exclaimed Kira. "It's pretty enough to be framed and hung on a wall." As she read, though, her brows wrinkled into a frown. "But the words aren't so pretty."

"What do they say?" Barbie asked.

Shaking her head in confusion, Kira translated for Barbie:

False claims of courage
Will bring to this family
Great shame and disgrace.

Kira went to get Mariko. When Mariko saw the note, her hand flew to her mouth. "Where did you find that note?"

Chapter Two

"It was on the floor in front of the teapot," Barbie answered. "It's a **haiku,** isn't it? A kind of Japanese poem?"

"Yes," Mariko answered, scanning the beautifully formed characters. "A poem, a mystery, and a cause for great concern."

A smiling, gray-haired man who stood very straight came over to them. He welcomed Kira and bowed politely to Barbie, introducing himself as Mariko's father. But his smile vanished when Mariko showed him the note. His eyebrows curved upward in alarm.

"'False claims of courage,'" Barbie repeated "It sounds as if someone is trying to cast doubt on your ancestor's story. But why?"

Mariko's face turned red. "I am not sure. But it is not the first time."

Her father shook his head, warning her not to say more. Barbie knew that in the Japanese culture, families often kept their problems to themselves.

Kira must have been thinking the same thing "We may be able to help," she said. "After all, I'r part of your family. And nobody is better than Barbie at solving mysteries."

Mariko placed her hand on her father's arm. "Please, Father."

He was silent for a minute. Finally he nodded "Yes, there have been other notes. Two others."

"What did they say?" Barbie asked gently.

Mariko looked at her father questioningly. Once again he nodded.

Mariko went to a wooden cupboard and opened the top drawer. Then she brought back two pieces of paper. They were covered with the same kind of calligraphy. The writing was as shaded and graceful as a painting. But again, the messages were troubling and puzzling.

Kira translated the notes for Barbie. The first one read:

Was Tomio brave?
Or the shameless inventor
Of a shameful lie?

Kira read the next one.

Something of value
That is selfishly guarded
Is truly worthless.

"Hmmm." Barbie thought about the meanings of the notes. "Tomio, a liar? The teapot, worthless?" She looked up. "Where and when did you find these?"

"One close to the entrance a few days ago,"

15

Mariko answered. "And one on an empty table in the back of the large room last week."

"Have you asked any of the waitresses about it?" asked Kira.

"No," said Mariko's father firmly. "Nor will we. This is a family matter." Just then the door opened and a heavyset young man rushed in. He looked angry and distracted as he ran his hand through his short, black hair. He stomped over to Mariko and her father.

Out of the corner of her eye, Barbie saw Teri, the waitress, hurry out of the room. She looked as if she expected trouble.

"This is **Hiro,**" Mariko said, introducing him to the women. "His mother and my father are cousins. Hiro and his mother own a small restaurant in downtown Kyoto. Hiro, meet our visitors, Barbie and Kira."

Hiro bowed very briefly to them and began speaking rapidly to Mariko's father. "As I have told you," Hiro began, "we are giving a very important party at our restaurant. Our guests would be honored by the presence of our ancestor's teapot. Such honor should be shared. May I tell my mother that you will lend us the teapot?"

Mariko's father spoke quietly. "Hiro, we have discussed this matter twice already. I will explain it to you a third time. The teapot has its place of honor in the Inn of Ten Blessings. Our ancestor always kept it in this place. We must show respect by keeping it here. To move it would dishonor our ancestor and our entire family. It would bring ill fortune."

Hiro's face flushed with anger. "Your selfishness will bring worse ill fortune!"

Mariko gasped. "Hiro! You must not speak to my father this way!"

Hiro's voice had become very loud. Several customers hurried past him, looking embarrassed to witness a family quarrel. Mariko tried to lead

Hiro to a corner of the room. But when she touched his sleeve, she dropped one of the haiku. Quickly, Hiro grabbed it.

"A shameful lie," Hiro read out loud. At first he looked puzzled. Then a mean smile spread across his face. "A shameful lie! Ha! It sounds as if someone thinks our ancestor's story is false. What a disgrace! I cannot wait to tell my mother—and everyone else I can find—that the 'honorable' teapot may be a fake!"

"Hiro!" Mariko cried. "Please!"

But Hiro was already out the door.

"I'm so sorry," Barbie said softly.

Mariko's father shrugged. "A family problem," he replied. "We will solve it."

Chapter Three

Mariko's father excused himself and walked away, his shoulders straight and proud. But Barbie guessed that he must be very upset.

Mariko shook her head, her lips set in a straight line. "It would be a disaster if Hiro started spreading this story. Do you think you can help us figure out what is going on before that happens?"

"Of course," Kira said.

"We will certainly try," Barbie agreed. "But we'll have to act fast. We're due in **Tokyo** for filming in two days. A crew is waiting for us, so we can't change the date. Right now we have to scout out some downtown Kyoto spots before it gets dark."

"I know you will do what you can," said Mariko. "Thank you."

They said good-bye and promised to return the next day. It was hard to leave knowing that Mariko and her father were so troubled. "Maybe by tomorrow we'll have some answers," Barbie thought with a sigh.

Like the Inn of Ten Blessings, downtown Kyoto was two worlds in one. Religious temples and shrines seemed to glow in the soft spring daylight. **Sushi** bars sold rice and raw fish rolled in

seaweed. But they stood next to American-style fast-food restaurants.

Barbie and Kira roamed around, taking pictures. They wrote down descriptions, **observations,** and addresses. After several hours, they stopped to rest in a park with a small fishpond. Black, speckled, and gold koi moved through the water. The gold ones flashed in the sun.

"I think we have enough background places to choose from," Kira stated, glancing at her notes. "Maybe we should think about the tableware now. We need to find just the right cups, bowls, and scoops for a formal tea setting. It would be nice to use some antiques."

"We passed an antique shop on a side street a while ago," Barbie said. "Let's go check it out."

The buildings looked run-down. But the shop's owner was quite the opposite. She wore expensive clothes and beautiful jewelry. Her long nails were polished scarlet. She seemed open and friendly as the two filmmakers explained what they needed.

"I have just finished setting up this tea display," she told them. She led them to a table. "You can take pictures and notes if you wish. But I need to rearrange something on that high shelf. Please excuse me."

The owner climbed up a ladder as Barbie and Kira examined the table setting. Smooth black bowls sat near smaller delicate cups. They saw a bamboo whisk. It looked like the one Mariko had used to stir their tea. Then they saw something else that they recognized from the Inn of Ten Blessings. It was a cast-iron teapot like the one at the teahouse. Only it had a gold lid.

"It looks just like the one at Mariko's teahouse," said Kira. "Except for the lid."

"And this teapot looks brand-new," Barbie pointed out.

"It *is* brand-new," called the owner. She was

22

high up on the ladder. "It is a copy of something very old and very rare: an emperor's teapot. Only a few of them were made. If this were the real thing, I could sell it for a small fortune."

Barbie wanted to ask the woman more. But just then the phone rang. The owner climbed down the ladder to answer it. Since she was on the phone for a while, Barbie and Kira left the shop.

"Do you think Mariko's teapot could be an emperor's?" asked Kira when they were outside.

"I don't know," Barbie admitted. "But that's one of the things I'd like to find out."

Chapter Four

The next day, Barbie and Kira got to the Inn of Ten Blessings before it opened. They wanted to take some pictures for their film. Right away, Barbie could tell something was wrong. Mariko seemed nervous. She kept glancing at the paneled section of the teahouse.

When the teahouse later opened, a man with gold-rimmed glasses came in. He walked directly to the teapot and stood before it, staring. Mariko joined him and brought Barbie and Kira over, too.

Mariko introduced them to Dr. Matsu, a

professor at the university. Everyone exchanged greetings. Mariko glanced again toward the paneled area. The others followed her gaze.

The shadows of three people could be seen through the paper panels: two men and one woman. One of the men was heavyset. The other man was slim and sitting very straight. The woman was seated between them.

The heavyset man stood up and began to wave his arms. The woman touched him on the shoulder, as if to calm him. The other man shrugged as if he had no more to say. A familiar angry voice drifted out.

"It's Hiro and his mother," Barbie thought, "along with Mariko's father."

Mariko frowned. Her cheeks were flushed. "Please excuse me," she said politely. "I will return shortly." She slid open the panels and went into the other room.

No one seemed to know what to say next.

So Barbie asked Dr. Matsu what he taught at the university.

"Writing," he informed her. "And one night a week I teach a class of poetry."

Kira shot a glance at Barbie. "Do you teach haiku?" she asked.

"Oh, yes," Dr. Matsu replied. "I not only teach haiku, I write it as well. I come here whenever I can because the teapot inspires me. I have done some of my best work right after making a visit. In fact, I wish I could keep the teapot with me always. Or at least I would like to come and visit more often."

"Why is that?" asked Barbie.

"There is a poetry prize being offered at the university," Dr. Matsu answered. "It is quite a lot of money. If I won it, I could take a trip to the mountain town of **Takayama.** Such a beautiful setting would inspire more poetry. It would be a dream come true!"

Just then, Teri, the waitress, passed by. She smiled and greeted Dr. Matsu. He nodded and waved. "He must come here often enough if Teri knows him," Barbie thought.

The professor excused himself, saying he had a class to teach. Barbie and Kira decided to have some tea and discuss their film. They found a table at the far end of the big room. The room was now noisy and crowded with customers. One of them was a slim woman in elegant clothing an expensive jewelry.

"Look!" Barbie whispered to Kira. "It's the owner of the antique shop."

The woman got up to leave. As they watche she walked across the room to view the teapot. She stopped for a few minutes, studying it. Then she shook her head sadly and left.

"Everyone seems to be interested in that teapot," Kira observed.

Barbie leaned forward, resting her chin on

her hands and thinking hard. "Yes. The question is who is interested in it enough to write these notes?"

Kira wrinkled her forehead. "That's what I don't understand, Barbie. Why would anyone who likes the teapot try to ruin its reputation? It doesn't make sense."

"Maybe it does," Barbie replied. "Maybe the antique dealer knows the teapot is an emperor's. Maybe she thinks Mariko's father would sell it to her if he thought its story was false."

"Hmmm. And Dr. Matsu might want it to inspire his poetry," added Kira. "But Hiro wants the teapot to bring in customers. Would customers still come to see a teapot whose story had been dishonored?"

"Probably not," said Barbie. "The writer may just be *threatening* to dishonor the teapot. Then that might force Mariko's father to quietly sell the teapot before anyone found out. The writer may not be planning to share his or her poems with anyone else."

Voices from the paneled area became louder. Hiro's voice rose above the others.

"Speaking of Hiro," Kira said, "he seems like the most obvious suspect. But I can't quite see him writing those haiku notes."

"You never can tell," Barbie reminded her.

Just then the panels flew open, and Hiro stomped out. Once again, Barbie noticed the waitress turn and leave the room when she saw him. Was she afraid of him?

That would not have surprised Barbie. Hiro was almost shouting now. An older woman rushed after him, clearly embarrassed. Then came Mariko and her father. Everyone tried to hush Hiro, but his angry words kept coming. Finally he and his mother put on their shoes and hurried out of the teahouse.

"It isn't like a Japanese family to argue in

front of strangers," Kira explained. "Hiro and his mother must be **desperate.**"

"I agree," said Barbie. "It seems as if they would do anything to get that teapot."

Mariko slowly approached their table. "I apologize for my family," she began. "It is not right to cause such a scene. I am very sad that my cousin is angry with us. But I must agree with my father. Our ancestor's teapot must stay here."

"There is no need to apologize," Kira replied gently. She patted Mariko's arm.

"It *must* be Hiro who is writing those notes," said Mariko sadly. "How terrible for a member of our family to behave this way."

Barbie stood up to leave. "We're going to track down some clues," she told Mariko. "Perhaps we will have some real answers soon."

On the way to the door, Barbie stopped for one last look at the teapot. Today the vase next

to it contained a
single branch of
cherry blossoms.
But just as before,
a piece of white
paper lay on the floor.

"Oh, no!" Barbie cried as Mariko picked
it up.

The paper was covered with Japanese
writing. It was formed in that same impressive
style. As Mariko read it, she shook her head in
disbelief. "This is the worst one yet," she said
softly. She handed it to Kira, who again translated

What starts the worst fire?
Not nature or accident
But one evil man.

"'An evil man!'" Barbie repeated in shock.
"The writer is actually saying Mariko's ancestor
started the fire!"

Chapter Five

Barbie and Kira decided to put their work on hold for the day. They wanted to revisit the antique dealer. They would also try to talk with Hiro and his mother. Mariko wrote down the address of Hiro's restaurant. Kira stuck the paper in her pocket.

A little while later, Barbie and Kira entered the antique shop. There they found the owner hard at work. Cartons were everywhere. She was making signs with prices and descriptions. A pile of finished signs was stacked behind the counter.

"Hello again," the store owner said to the

women. "Excuse me for being so busy with packing. For some time, I have been trying to buy a shop across town. This morning I was told the deal had gone through. So I am moving. This neighborhood has changed. I think my business could do better elsewhere."

"We're glad for your good fortune," Kira said. "By the way, we saw you earlier—at the Inn of Ten Blessings."

"Yes, I love to go there," the store owner replied. "The teapot seems to have a special power that calms me." She smiled. "I offered the owners a lot of money to buy it. No one knows whether it's an emperor's or not. So I couldn't get much money for it. I thought it would make an interesting piece for the store. But the owners refused."

"Why can't you tell if it's an emperor's teapot?" asked Barbie curiously.

The dealer pointed to the lid of the teapot in

the display. "See this lid? Real emperors' teapots have solid gold ones. But the lid of the teapot at the inn has been missing for years. Now, if you will excuse me, I must get back to work."

The woman turned around. Kira and Barbie quickly glanced at the pile of finished signs behind the counter. The calligraphy didn't match the style on the haiku notes.

"The writing is completely different," whispered Kira. "Do you think we've just lost a suspect?"

"Maybe," Barbie whispered back. "But look outside!"

Through the window, they could see Hiro. He was wheeling a garbage can to the curb across the street. They watched in surprise as he entered a nearby building.

Kira pulled out the piece of paper with the address Mariko had written down. "That must be his restaurant!" she exclaimed. "But it looks so run-down and shabby."

The small building was in bad shape. Paint was peeling off the outside. The wooden steps sagged. A broken window was patched with cardboard.

The antique dealer heard them and shook her head sadly. "It used to be a nice place, but then the neighborhood changed. Also, the mother was ill for a while. And they lost business."

Barbie and Kira thanked the owner and said good-bye. Then they stepped outside. The shabby restaurant looked sad and deserted.

"They may need more than a famous teapot to save their business," Kira commented.

The women carefully walked across the wooden porch, stepping around some broken planks. They knocked on the door. No one answered. They tried to open it, but it was locked.

"Not expecting customers," Kira guessed.

"How could they be planning to give a big, fancy party here?"

"Perhaps that was just a story Hiro made up," Barbie answered softly. "How sad. One last attempt to get the teapot."

Suddenly the door flew open with a bang. Hiro stood there, his eyes flashing. His mouth was set in a grim, angry line. His frown deepened as he recognized Barbie and Kira. "What do you want?" he growled.

Chapter Six

"May we come in?" asked Barbie steadily.

Hiro gave a short, unpleasant laugh. "Why?" he asked. "So you can go back and tell my cousin how bad business is?"

Behind him, a soft voice spoke. Hiro muttered and stepped aside. His mother motioned for Barbie and Kira to come in. Hiro returned to his place behind the sushi bar.

The inside of the small restaurant was airy and clean like Mariko's. But some of the chairs had missing rungs. The tables were scratched and scarred. Few of the dishes matched. The paper on the paneled screen was torn and patched.

Still, Barbie could detect the fragrance of raw fish and **vinegared** rice. She mentioned how much she loved sushi to Hiro's mother.

Hiro's mother bowed and smiled. "My son is a great cook. He is the best sushi chef in all of Kyoto. Even better than I am. He could be a chef anywhere. But he has stayed here, trying to make our business better. While I was ill, we lost many customers."

They could see Hiro at the bar, slicing fish.

"If you are serving lunch, we would love to stay," Barbie suggested.

"We're starved," agreed Kira.

"Please, you must be our guests," said Hiro's mother. She led them to a spot at the counter. "You must forgive my son's rudeness at the Inn of Ten Blessings. It was a family matter. We should not

have spoiled your visit there."

They sat down and watched Hiro work. His frown began to soften. In a few minutes, he handed Barbie and Kira a wooden platter. It held an arrangement of pink and white sliced fish over neat blocks of white rice. Another platter held tiny, bright orange eggs wrapped in seaweed. Hiro's sushi truly was the best they had ever tasted.

At his mother's suggestion, Hiro sat down with the two women. As they praised his food, Barbie noticed the beginnings of a smile on his face. "I apologize for my earlier behavior," he finally said. "My mother has worked hard for many years. When she was ill, it was difficult to keep things running. And by the time she was better, customers had stopped coming because of the neighborhood. We need something special to bring people back—something like the teapot."

"The teapot brings honor and good fortune," his mother agreed. "But it belongs to the other side of the family."

"But Hiro's cooking doesn't belong to the other side of the family!" Barbie cried. "Why don't you expand into a bigger, full-scale restaurant?"

Hiro shook his head. "We once hoped to do that. But it would cost too much money. We would need to pay for repairs, cooking equipment, furniture . . ." He stood up. "I must clean up now. Once again, I am sorry for my rudeness."

"And once again, we thank you for a truly wonderful meal," Barbie said.

"The finest in Kyoto!" added Kira.

After Hiro left, his mother gave them a tired smile. "Borrowing the teapot was our last chance. Now my son will have to find work elsewhere. We had such hopes. I even had menus made up, listing all his special dishes. I have been saving them for the day we opened a full-scale restaurant. I have not shown them to anyone, not even Hiro."

She took a scroll of paper from a drawer

and unrolled it. Barbie and Kira gasped. They recognized the calligraphy at once. It was the same delicate, beautiful writing as on the haiku!

"This was going to be a surprise. One of our waitresses wrote it for me," Hiro's mother continued. "She worked on it whenever we had slow times. Then there were so many slow times that she had to find other work. Doesn't she have beautiful writing?"

"Yes, she does," Kira agreed. She glanced over at Barbie. "Where does she work now?"

"I do not know," Hiro's mother answered.

Suddenly Barbie had an idea. "I think we might," she said slowly. She turned to the older woman. "Can you and Hiro close up and come with us now? Just for a little while?"

"But where and why?" asked Hiro's mother.

"To help solve a mystery once and for all," said Barbie. "And perhaps to help save a family."

Chapter Seven

When the foursome arrived at the Inn of Ten
Blessings, there weren't many customers. But Dr.
Matsu was at his favorite spot, sipping tea and
studying the teapot. Mariko and her father looked
worried when they saw their relatives. But Barbie
assured them that everything was fine. Hiro
apologized for his earlier behavior.

It was a warm afternoon. So the group decided
to slide the screens open and sit outside. From the
deck, they could see the pond. Barbie quietly asked
Mariko if Teri could serve them. Mariko looked
puzzled, but she sent for the waitress.

In a few minutes, Teri came out with tea and cakes. Hiro jumped to his feet. "Teri!" he cried in surprise. "I did not know you worked here!"

"Nor did I!" his mother exclaimed.

"You know one another?" asked Mariko's father.

"Yes," replied Teri, looking from one person to another. She seemed nervous and upset. She brushed back her hair and stared at the ground. "I worked for Hiro and his mother before coming here. I did not tell you because I knew there were bad feelings between the families. I chose not to be in the middle of them."

The group sat quietly for a minute. Then Hiro broke the silence by asking Teri how her studies were going.

"Which studies?" Kira asked.

"I am studying poetry at night at the university," Teri explained. "Dr. Matsu is helping me."

"So that's how you knew Dr. Matsu," Barbie

48

said. "Do your studies with Dr. Matsu include haiku?"

Teri looked down again. She gave a nod.

Barbie hated to ask, but they all had to know. "Teri, did you write the haiku about Mariko's ancestor?" she asked gently.

Tears slipped from the young woman's eyes. She nodded again. "I did not mean to make things worse," Teri began. "The first time Hiro came here, I did not want him to see me. I felt that I should have stayed and worked for him, even though business was bad. I should have tried to help him and his mother. I heard him asking to borrow the teapot. And I thought of a way I *could* help." She brushed her tears away. "I knew it was wrong. But I thought I could make Mariko's father believe the story was not true. Then he might let Hiro borrow the teapot. The family would come together again. And Hiro's small restaurant might do better."

No one made a sound as Teri continued her story. "That night I wrote the first haiku. I dropped it where I knew Mariko would find it." Teri sighed. "But when Hiro returned, I saw that the first haiku had not helped. I tried again and then two more times. Nothing helped. Instead, the poems have done more harm than good. I have dishonored myself and your family, Mariko. I will prepare to leave your teahouse."

Mariko's father shook his head. "We have dishonored the family ourselves, Teri. You were only trying to right our wrong."

Hiro stood up. "Thank you for trying to help us, Teri," he said. "But I am tired of fighting about the teapot. I will not let it cause more damage to our family. We will not ask for it again."

Mariko's father stood, too. "Hiro," he stated. "I see now that I have been wrong. Our honorable ancestor would have wanted me to share the teapot's blessings with family. From now on, we *will* share it. You can have it half the year, and we will have it the other half."

"That is most generous!" exclaimed Hiro's mother. "Thank you! I am sure it will bring us blessings and luck."

Barbie's eyes sparkled. "May I suggest something else that might bring blessings and luck? Perhaps the Inn of Ten Blessings could be expanded. Mariko has told us that customers keep asking for a fuller menu. Hiro could be the chef. His mother could help Mariko's father manage it. That way the teapot doesn't have to leave the place of your ancestor. And Hiro can do the work he loves."

"And is so good at!" added Kira.

"What a wonderful idea!" cried Mariko.

But her father wasn't so sure. "True, it is a wonderful idea," he said. "However, it is also a very expensive idea. We would need to remodel our kitchen and add more servers."

Everyone was silent. Barbie stared out at the pond, looking for answers. A gold gleam caught her eye. "How strange," she thought. "There are only dark koi in the inn's pond, not gold ones." She decided to walk down to the pond to take a closer look.

Suddenly Barbie ran back to the deck. She held a dripping object in her hand. A sparkle of gold gleamed through a thick coating of mud.

Teri got a towel and wiped off the mud and leaves that clung to it. Soon something incredible emerged. Everyone gasped. "It's the lid of a teapot," Kira cried. "And it *is* solid gold!"

"An emperor's teapot," Mariko declared. "The lid must have risen to the surface when the pond was being cleaned last week."

Mariko turned to her father. "This is very valuable! We have the money to expand after all!"

Mariko's father was smiling broadly. "We will never sell our brave ancestor's teapot, with or without the lid," he explained. "But I believe our bank will now lend us money based on the new value of the teapot."

"Word of my son's talent will soon spread. The increased business will help us pay back the money quickly," said Hiro's mother proudly.

The family laughed and celebrated their good fortune. Teri brought out more tea and cakes.

Barbie happily watched the newly united family. She whispered to Kira, "You know, I don't think we should call our film *The Way of Tea.*"

"Really?" Kira asked, surprised.

Barbie smiled. "No. I think we should call it *The Way of Family.*"